Aaliyah the Architect builds a mall.

She draws buildings,
big and small.

SUPER MALL
Is the cheese shop ready?

Brooke the Beekeeper tends to her bees.

They make tasty honey! Could we have some, please?

Charlotte the Chef is cooking some stew...

...if you're very lucky, she'll share it with you!

Dena the Dinosaur Hunter creeps through the grass.

She'll catch a T-Rex to show to her class.

Eve the Electrician fixes our lights.

She makes sure that
they shine bright!

You want me to
stick this where?

Fatima is a Forensic Scientist, looking for hints.

She's gathering clues
and fingerprints.

You may as well give up now!

Grace the Gardener pulls up weeds...

She'll take them all out and plant flower seeds.

Shower time!
I brought my
own soap.

Heidi the Helicopter Pilot soars so high!

She spends her days way up in the sky.

Izzy the Inventor makes new things.

Her favorite inventions have whirligigs and wings!

Julieta the Judge knows right from wrong.

She makes big decisions all day long.

Just call me Rusty.
Hon. J. Garcia

Keiko the Knight has a horse named Dutch.

She'll do her own rescuing, thank you very much.

Yeah, that's right!

Lily loves working as
a Lighthouse Keeper.

She makes sure boats stay
where water is deeper.

Surf's up!

Mila the Mathematician knows 2 + 2...

She can multiply, subtract, and do long division, too!

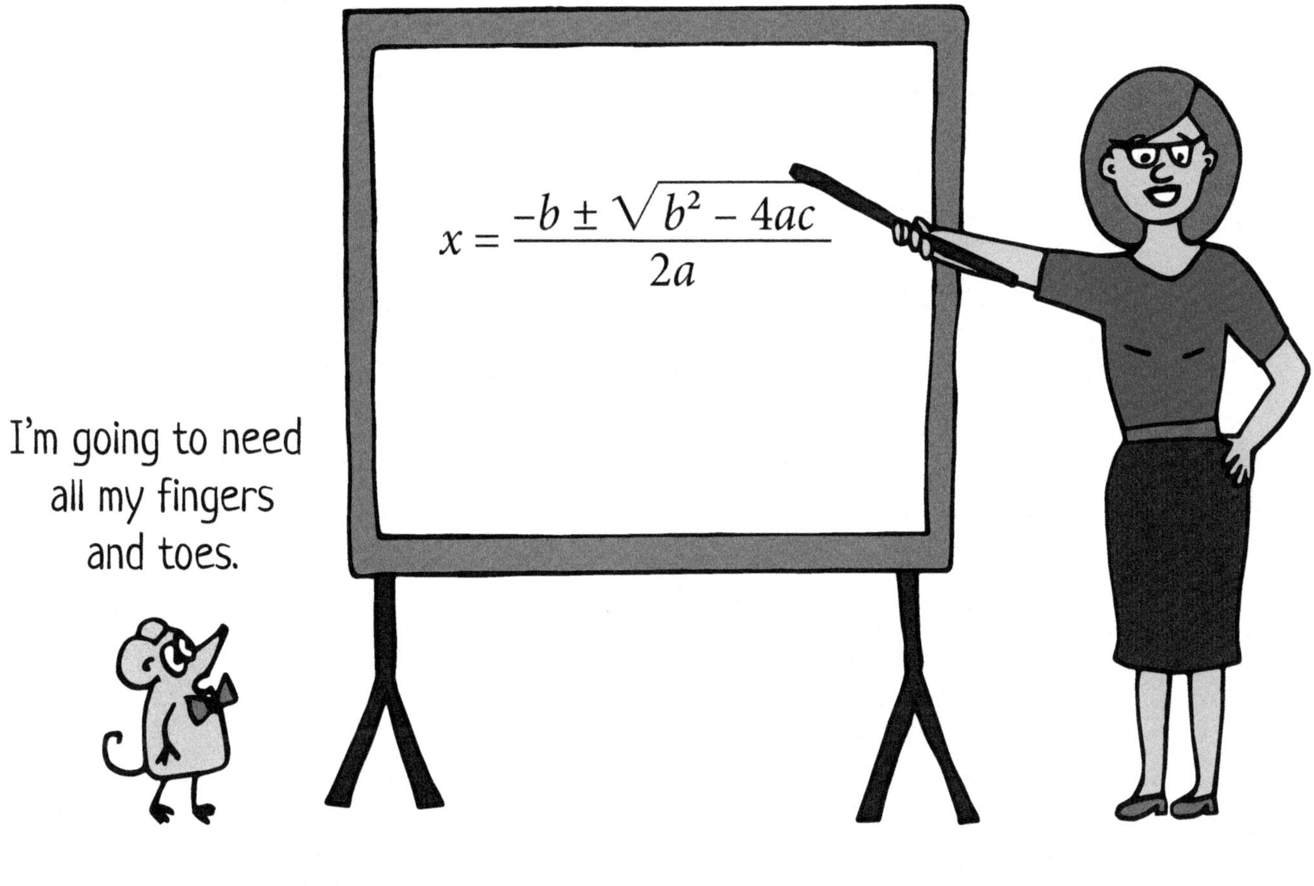

Nova the Noodle Taster eats all day long.

She spins noodles on her fork and hums silly songs!

Olivia the Oceanographer works on a boat.

She studies dolphins and whales, but never a goat!

Penny the Plumber fixes pipes the right way.

She'll come with her tools to save the day!

You're going to put a snake where now?

Queisha the Queen plans to quit her job.

She hates sitting around on the throne like a blob.

We're opening an accounting firm.

Ritu the Robotics Engineer
built a new pal.

A shiny new robot and she named it Sal.

Yes but can
he make me a
cheese sandwich?

Simone the Surgeon will fix your boo-boo.

She'll stitch up your teddy
if he needs it too!

Hey, eyes down here.
I'm still the cutest
one in this book.

Tatiana the Train Conductor wears a special hat.

And she never listens to people who say, “Girls can’t do that!”

All aboard to Cheesetown!

Ursula the Urban Planner makes her mark.

She'll find the best place for a playground or park.

And this is where the cheese factories will go.

Vida the Veterinarian is fixing a budgie.

She'll help you as well if your cat gets too pudgy.

There is no way this ends well.

Willow the Web Designer has a job in the city.

She makes websites that work and are also so pretty!

www.cheesesandwiches.com?

Xiaojing is a musician who plays the Xylophone.

She can play with a band or even alone.

I'll shake it 'til I break it.

Yazmin the Yoga Teacher says "namaste."

She teaches us to bend and stretch every day.

I think I pulled my namaste.

Zoey the Zamboni Driver loves to see you skate.

The game can't start without her,
so she better not be late!

Laura Hamilton is a mother of one, who is prone to occasional bouts of rage in book stores when confronted with the wall of princess books. Her daughter may have a tiara, but she's really handy with a hammer. During the day, she works in health care research. At night, she's in bed by 8 pm.

Cheryl Cook is a long time doodler who is far too suggestible, especially when around Laura. She likes wine, cooking, and long walks on the beach. By day, she's an interior decorator. By night, she watches too many British crime dramas.

CPSIA information can be obtained
at www.ICGtesting.com
Printed in the USA
LVOW05s0153281016
510604LV00014B/110/P

9 780995 337015